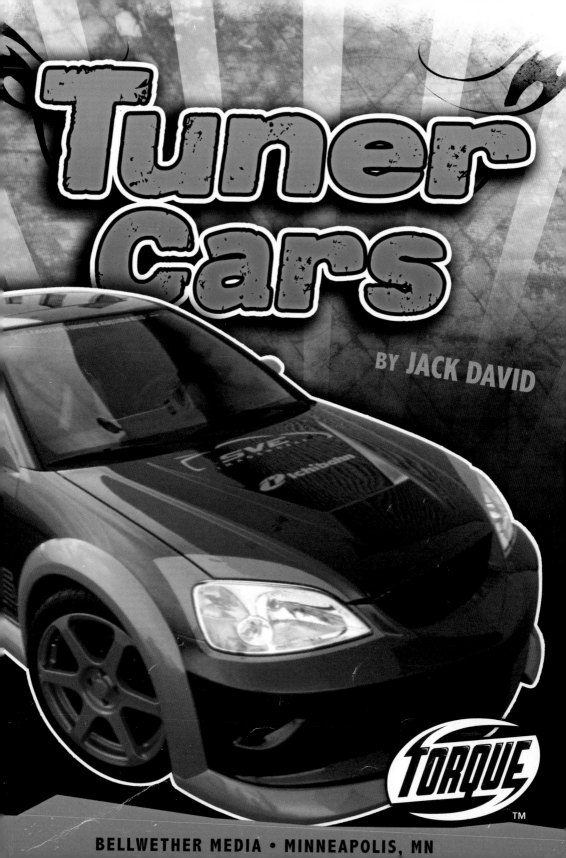

Tuner Cars

BY JACK DAVID

BELLWETHER MEDIA • MINNEAPOLIS, MN

TORQUE ™

Are you ready to take it to the extreme?
Torque books thrust you into the action-packed world
of sports, vehicles, and adventure. These books may
include dirt, smoke, fire, and dangerous stunts.

WARNING: READ AT YOUR OWN RISK.

This edition first published in 2008 by Bellwether Media.

No part of this publication may be reproduced in whole or in part without written
permission of the publisher. For information regarding permission, write to
Bellwether Media Inc., Attention: Permissions Department, Post Office Box 19349,
Minneapolis, MN 55419.

Library of Congress Cataloging-in-Publication Data

David, Jack, 1968-
 Tuner cars / by Jack David.
    p. cm. -- (Torque--cool rides)
 Summary: "Full color photography accompanies engaging information about
Tuner Cars. The combination of high-interest subject matter and light text is
intended for students in grades 3 through 7"--Provided by publisher.
 Includes bibliographical references and index.
 ISBN-13: 978-1-60014-154-6 (hardcover : alk. paper)
 ISBN-10: 1-60014-154-4 (hardcover : alk. paper)
 1. Hot rods--Juvenile literature. 2. Automobiles--Performance--Juvenile
literature. I. Title.

 TL236.3.D385 2008
 629.222'1--dc22

                                                              2007040568

Contents

What Is a Tuner Car?

Tuner cars are fast, sleek, and cool. Their owners want to have the nicest car on the road.

Tuner cars are **sport compact cars** that have been modified to improve their performance. Owners make changes to the engine and body to get acceleration and speed. Small, powerful cars such as the Honda Civic and the Toyota Supra are popular for tuner cars. The cars most frequently turned into tuner cars have been from Japanese automakers. However, any sport compact model can be turned into a tuner.

Fast FaCt

The term "tuner" can refer to either the tuner car itself or the person who modifies it.

Tuner Car History

Tuner car owners have one basic goal. They want to modify a factory-made car to make it faster and more unique. Car owners have been doing this since the 1920s. Early Model T Ford owners turned their cars into **hot rods**.

Tuner cars weren't widely known until 2001. That was the year the film *The Fast and the Furious* arrived at theaters across the United States. The movie showed the tuner car culture as exciting and *The Fast and the Furious* set off a wave of interest in tuner cars.

Fast FaCt

Many owners "shave" their tuner cars by removing parts such as bumpers, door handles, and trim. This gives the car a smooth, sleek look and also reduces wind resistance.

Tuner Car Parts

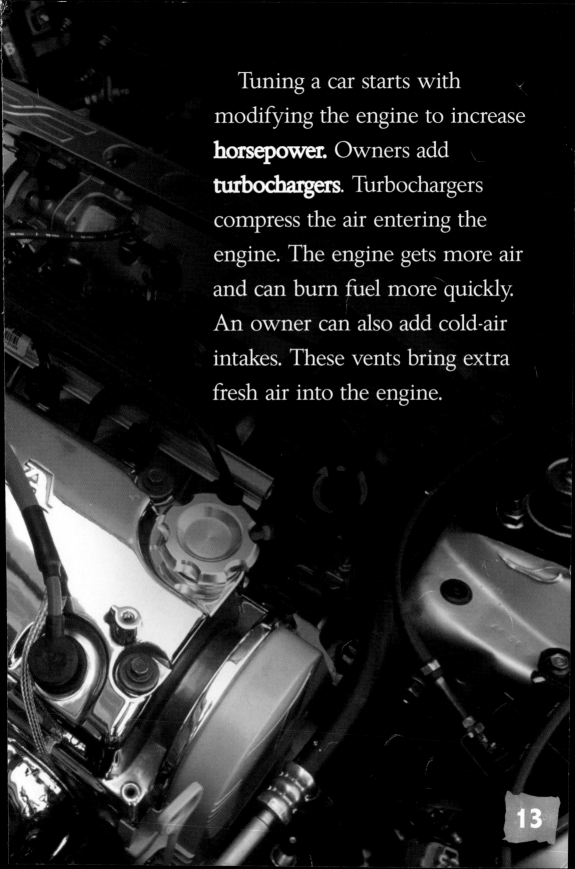

Tuning a car starts with modifying the engine to increase **horsepower.** Owners add **turbochargers**. Turbochargers compress the air entering the engine. The engine gets more air and can burn fuel more quickly. An owner can also add cold-air intakes. These vents bring extra fresh air into the engine.

Adding tanks of **nitrous oxide** (nitro) is another way to increase horsepower. A car's engine can burn nitro much faster than it burns gasoline. Therefore, nitro provides much more horsepower than gasoline. However, using nitro can be dangerous.

Owners also tune the suspension system. They add short springs that allow the cars to ride low to the ground. **Sway bars** improve handling. They balance a car's weight during turns.

Fast FaCt

Some Japanese automakers provide less powerful cars to North America than they do in other parts of the world. Some owners tune a car by bringing it up to the performance of worldwide models.

Owners also tune the body. Some body tuning is just for appearance. Other changes can affect performance. **Spoilers** are wing-shaped parts attached to the rear of a car. Air presses the spoiler down and keeps the back of the car on the ground. This gives the rear tires better grip.

Tuner Cars in Action

Tuner car owners love to show off their cars. Some enter cars in custom car shows. These shows feature tuner cars as well as other kinds of modified cars.

Fast FaCt

Many tuners like to add doors that open from the front instead of the back. These "suicide doors" are extremely dangerous. Front-opening doors, if not tightly closed, can get ripped wide open by the wind while the car is moving at high speed. Passengers could easily fall out.

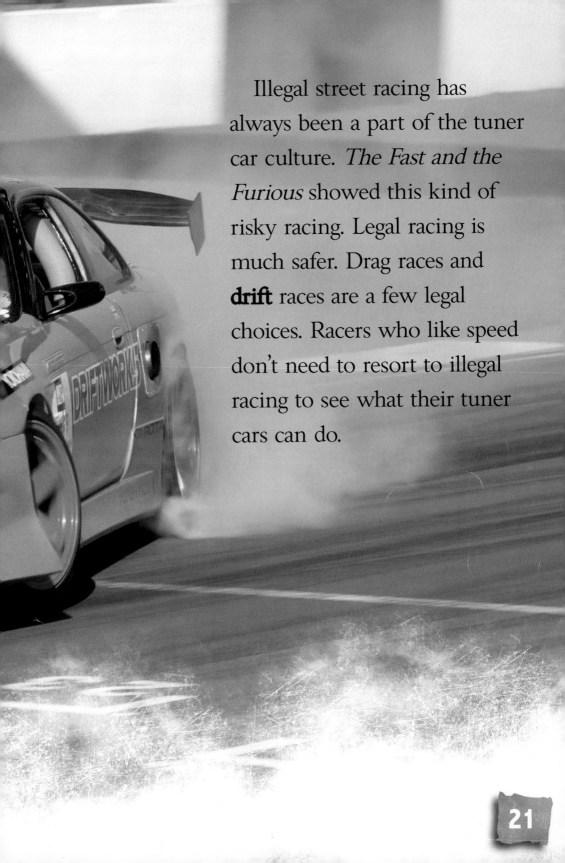

Illegal street racing has always been a part of the tuner car culture. *The Fast and the Furious* showed this kind of risky racing. Legal racing is much safer. Drag races and **drift** races are a few legal choices. Racers who like speed don't need to resort to illegal racing to see what their tuner cars can do.

Glossary

drift–to drive a car sharply in a turn so that the rear tires slide, or drift, and the front tires point in the direction opposite the turn

horsepower–a measure of an engine's power

hot rod–an early customized car featuring improved speed and a unique appearance

nitrous oxide–an explosive chemical used as a fuel additive to get huge bursts of speed

spoiler–the system of springs and shock absorbers that connects a tuner car's frame to its wheels

sport compact car–a class of small, high-performance cars

sway bar–part of a car's suspension that reduces the amount a car leans, or rolls, while in a sharp turn; a sway bar is also called a stabilizer bar or anti-roll bar.

turbocharger–an engine part on a tuner car that compresses the air entering the engine

To Learn More

AT THE LIBRARY

Braun, Eric. *Hot Rods*. Minneapolis, Minn.: Lerner, 2006.

Doeden, Matt. *Sports Cars*. Mankato, Minn.: Capstone, 2005.

Schuette, Sarah L. *Tuner Cars*. Mankato, Minn.: Capstone, 2006.

ON THE WEB

Learning more about tuner cars is as easy as 1, 2, 3.

1. Go to www.factsurfer.com

2. Enter "tuner cars" into search box.

3. Click the "Surf" button and you will see a list of related web sites.

With factsurfer.com, finding more information is just a click away.

Index